For Judy, Jennifer, Nyssa, and Emily
—the women in my life—
and for my son Ian,
who already knows.

BEAR

John Schoenherr

Philomel Books
New York

He woke in the cold rain and rolled onto the warm spot where his mother slept. Her scent was weak and the spot was cold. He sat straight up and took a deep whiff. She was gone!

He could smell the trees and the grass and the river and the mountains. There was no fresh smell of mother. He whimpered as he smelled harder and harder, but couldn't find his mother.

He ran up and down the trails they used, but there was no sign of her. All his life mother had been near him, finding food and protecting him. Now she was gone.

All afternoon he searched and got very hungry. He stopped to nibble at some berries, but they were green and sour. When he tried to dig up some bulbs, a lemming bit him on the nose. It hurt so much that he turned and ran down the hillside.

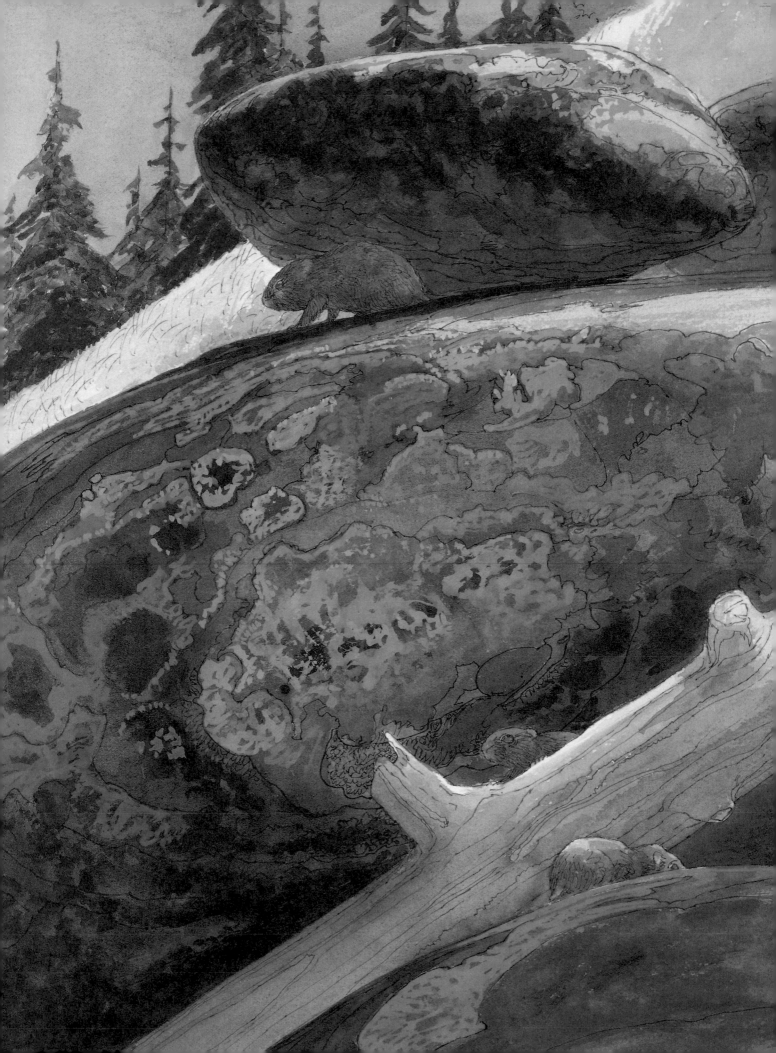

He found a trail in the deep moss of the spruce forest and followed it, fearfully, without his mother. He had never been here before.

A mother moose charged from behind some boulders and chased him away, back into the dark woods. He did not know where he was. Alone, he curled up and went to sleep.

The next morning he found another trail and followed it. He snuffled and whimpered and walked for days over mountains and snowfields and valleys of ash where nothing grew and there was nothing to eat.

Then one night he wandered hungrily into a new forest,
where a black shadow growled and charged toward him.
He ran without stopping until he climbed a tree on top of
a steep sandy slope. The big shadow circled and growled
and clawed for a long time. Finally it left. He whimpered
until he fell asleep, hugging the cold tree.

When morning came he was hungrier than ever, and thirsty. But a way down at the bottom of the moraine he could see a stream flowing. He carefully looked around his tree, and climbed down. Then he ran and slipped and tumbled down the steep shifting sands, right into the icy water.

The water was cold, but it smelled good. It was full of fish, and he saw their backs in the shallows. Big, bright, red, fat salmon!

They swam upstream by dozens and dozens and filled the pool with scarlet.

He charged after the nearest one but it got away easily.
He ran after all of them until the water was foamy and he
was tired, but he couldn't catch even one.

He put his face underwater and tried to sneak up on them. He sneaked faster and faster until he was like a moving wave. All he got was hungrier.

The sun was high in the sky when he climbed a rock in the middle of the stream and saw one last fish! He stood on his hind legs, let out an angry, hungry, tired roar, and jumped through the air onto it!

Now he knew how to fish! For weeks more fish came upstream, and he caught as many as he wanted. He grew bigger and stronger, and his roar got deeper and deeper as he grew. He chased sea gulls and even eagles from his pool.

And when the great dark shadow came to steal fish, he stood up on his hind legs and let out his deepest growl. The old bear ran away and never came back.

When the salmon stopped coming, he ate ripe berries that covered the hillsides. He had long forgotten his mother, but he was bigger and fatter and fiercer than ever—ready for winter and anything else.

Copyright © 1991 by John Schoenherr.
Published in 1991 by Philomel Books,
a division of The Putnam and Grosset Book Group.
200 Madison Avenue, New York, NY 10016.
All rights reserved.   Published simultaneously in Canada.
Printed in Hong Kong by South China Printing Co. (1988) Ltd.
The text is set in Administer Roman. Book design by Nanette Stevenson. Second Impression
Library of Congress Cataloging-in-Publication Data   Schoenherr, John.   Bear/by John Schoenherr.   p.cm.
Summary: Searching for his mother, a young bear finds his own independence.   1. Bears—Juvenile fiction.
[1. Bears—Fiction.]   I. Title.   PZ10.3.S29894Be   1990   [E]—dc20   89-26634 CIP AC   ISBN 0-399-22177-8